The MAGIC ARK

Brian Price-Thomas

HODDER AND STOUGHTON
LONDON SYDNEY AUCKLAND TORONTO

There was a hole in the fence at the bottom of my Nana's garden. On the other side was Mr Antrobus's yard.

Mr Antrobus made things. He wore a tall top hat and a frock coat. When he sawed wood, the sawdust never seemed to get onto his clothes.

In the corner of the yard was a big Noah's Ark. Sometimes, when I watched through the fence, the animals walked by themselves.

I always wanted to go into Mr Antrobus's yard,
but I knew it was not polite to go where you had not been asked.

One day I found two beetles and, pretending that they were two of
the Noah's Ark animals, I called to Mr Antrobus and told him I thought
they might be small tigers escaped from his yard.

"You are a very perceptive boy," he said.

I did not know what he meant, but his old eyes smiled
and I knew it was not a bad thing to be.

I do not remember the first time I saw the Ark floating above the ground. I must have been very small because I cannot remember being surprised.

There was a day when I was walking with Nana to the village. Mr Antrobus came floating over the hedge in the Ark just behind us, and he raised his hat to me. When I caught up with Nana I asked her,

"Why does Mr Antrobus raise his hat?"

"I cannot think what you are talking about," she replied.

It was no good asking Nana about things when she was like that.

It must have been not long after that when,
very early one morning, I saw from my window Mr Antrobus
riding in the Ark over the hedge by our garden gate.

    After the Ark had passed, I saw that there were roses growing just
where it had touched the hedge. At no other place could I see
even one petal.

At breakfast I said to Nana, "Why are there roses on our hedge?"

"Roses?" she said and looked at Grandad. "Why should there not be roses?"

Grandad said, "Don't you remember?"

"Remember? What is there to remember?" said Nana and turned back to the stove.

"Ah well," said Grandad, and he looked far far away as if there was a window in the wall he was staring at.

Later Nana picked the roses and put them in a vase where they stayed fresh for nearly as long as forever.

On my sixth birthday, Mr Antrobus called me to come to him through the fence. He was holding a small ladder with carved and painted swans' heads.

"This is your sixth birthday," he said.

"How do you know?" I asked.

"Are there not six rungs on the ladder?" he asked. I counted them and saw that there were.

I took the ladder home and showed it to Nana and Grandad.

"Whatever next?" said Nana, but Grandad stroked the swans' heads and smiled at them for a little while before I took the ladder to my room.

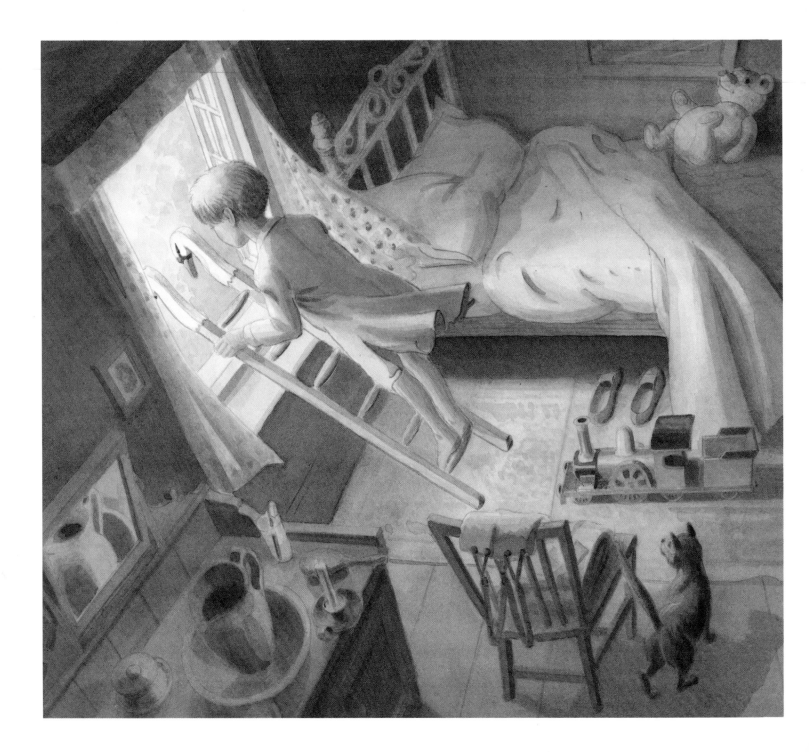

It was the summer time and I was always awake before the sun was.
I looked at my ladder and saw it was floating above the floor.

"Like the Noah's Ark," I thought.

The ladder floated to the side of my bed, so I got up
and climbed on to it.

The floor seemed to be floating underneath me.
I looked at the window and it started to
come towards me.

The garden, soft and secret, floated below me.
In his yard, Mr Antrobus was waiting for me.
He put aside my ladder, opened the doors of the Ark
and lowered its gangplank.

Out of his workshop came a long line of wooden animals.
Mr Antrobus went down to meet them and watched as they walked
two by two up into the Ark.

When the last of the animals were inside, Mr Antrobus pulled up the
gangplank and closed the doors before coming to stand beside me.

As we stood on the deck,
the ground below us began to pass by.
    I saw first the lane to the village,
then the duckpond beside the farm.
    More and more quickly the ground passed
under us.
    "Why does the ground go so fast?" I asked.
    "Because the world is young in the morning," Mr Antrobus replied.
    The sun shone over us from the distant edge of the world
and I saw that it was.

I moved to look down over the side of the Ark,
but instead the world tipped up slowly on its side
and passed beside us.

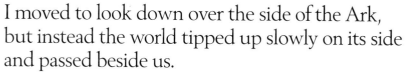

    "How does the world turn on its side?" I asked.
    "Are you sure that it has?" Mr Antrobus asked.
    "But the Ark always feels as if it isn't moving," I said.
    "Sometimes things are not as they seem."
    "It sounds like a riddle," I said.
    "Perhaps it is," Mr Antrobus said and he smiled.

After a time,
or perhaps it was no time at all,
the world tilted back and stopped still.

"It isn't a bit like home," I said,
looking at a forest that seemed to stretch
as far as the sunrise.

Then the ground rose up until high trees
were all around us, and the floor of the forest
touched the bottom of the Ark very gently.

Mr Antrobus opened the doors of the Ark and put down the gangplank.

Two by two, some of the animals came out of the Ark – first the squirrels, then the polecats, the wolves, the two bears, and last, the reindeer.

As they walked into the trees, the shadows seemed to soften them, and they became larger and furry.

The elephants came out through the doors, but Mr Antrobus called to them,

"Not yet, little ones, not yet!"

So they turned back, and when the doors were shut, the ground floated away and the world turned faster and faster.

Next time, the world stopped under a hot sky. Around the Ark
stretched a great plain of tall grass and small trees which, in the distance,
seemed to melt into the bottom of the sky.

This time, when the elephants came out, Mr Antrobus smiled
and nodded to them.
They were followed by the lions, the giraffes, the rhinoceroses
and other animals, all two by two.

Away into the tall grasses they walked,
and as they did so, the warmth of the morning
softened away the sharpness
of their wooden sides.

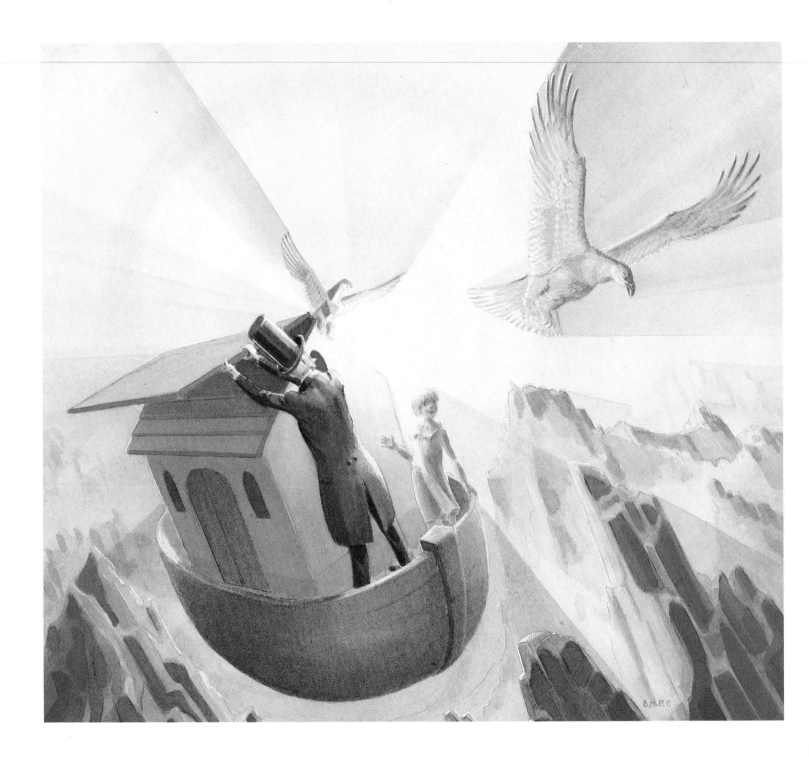

When the world next stopped, there were high mountains below us.

This time Mr Antrobus did not put down the gangplank, but opened the roof.

Two wooden eagles climbed out on to the edge. They unfolded their wooden wings and one after the other jumped into the air.

As I watched them sail into the sunbeams, their feathers spread like gold on their wings and sent them soaring away into the sky far above.

"Where is it to be now?" I asked. Mr Antrobus just smiled. When I looked down from his face I saw we were in the field behind our garden. Mr Antrobus only let out two sheep and two rabbits.

"There are still lots more animals inside. Are they to come out too?"

But as I spoke I heard the chickens in our yard and I knew the day had begun.

"Why isn't the world young all the time?" I cried.

"Have patience, little one," said Mr Antrobus, and he gave me a little basket. "Pick mushrooms for your Nana," he said.

"Are there mushrooms here?" I asked.

As I stepped down from the Ark, I saw that there were mushrooms everywhere.

British Library Cataloguing in Publication Data

Price-Thomas, Brian
   The magic ark.
   I. Title
   823′.914[J]   PZ7
   ISBN 0-340-40422-1

First published 1987

Published by Hodder and Stoughton Children's Books,
a division of Hodder and Stoughton Ltd,
Mill Road, Dunton Green, Sevenoaks, Kent TN13 2YJ

Printed in Great Britain by Purnell and Sons Ltd, Paulton (Bristol) and London
Member of the BPCC Group